Kas

DIARY

LATOYA LIKAMBI

THE DIARY OF KASEY

AND HER LIFE

the Anderson family!!!

Kasey's DIARY

LATOYA LIKAMBI

POPULAR

LONDON

School

NEW TEACHER

AVA + EVA = DOUBLE TROUBLE

14

Other Books by the Author:

Short Stories by Latoya Likambi

ISBN

Hardcover: 9780368630491

Softcover: 9780368630507

DEDICATION

To my siblings, God sisters & God brothers, cousins, and friends… This book is dedicated to you all with love!

Love, Latoya xxxx

PROLOGUE

Welcome to my (Kasey Elena Anderson's) personal diary. Whoever reads this is in for a weird, surprising treat. My diary is full of fun, weird, and bubbly stuff. It is about my hectic, hilarious, cringe-worthy, and fun life. It contains my six best friends: Sophie, Patricia, Laura, Katy, Chloe, and Alisha.

We call ourselves the *cool humble weird* girls. Be prepared to laugh, yawn, and freak out whilst reading. Hope you enjoy the read… Oh, and you are my special fan-friends too!

CHAPTER ONE

THE ORDINARY DRAMA FEST

I was with Laura and Sophie. It was so hot and boring after a morning at Sophie's house, helping with the spring-cleaning. We were on our way to the local town pool to meet up with the rest of the *cool humble weird* girls. On the way, we took Katy along, who was hanging out with Jay and Blake. Just then (obviously), we HAD come across Brittney and her popular petty group... Just great! They were going swimming too! She was the popular queen bee school bully who snatched great opportunities away from us, turned everyone's lives into shambles, sabotaged my privacy, and was just mean in general.

Suddenly, she barged into Katy and me. "OMG, HI. My little sister has that sweater!" he gushed.

"Ok?" I said, confused as to why she was quite nice to me.

Then she flicked her hair and scoffed, "But actually, she uses it to wipe her en suite floor!"

"Seriously," I groaned, "she is so mean! What type of loathsome, nauseating bigmouth does that? She should just keep her thoughts to herself."

Later on, after a great deal of embarrassment, she and her pack went back home, hopefully to fix their wacky hair extensions or get their nails done. Come on, we all know that she had more acrylics than brains☺.

But at least we got to have a peaceful swim and hang out afterwards.

***

The summer days quickly slipped by and special people passed away (okay, right now I sound so tender and slushy). In addition to that, Katy and Laura got these new clients for their architect design job (which is just a temporary summer job to earn a few dollars). It is not as professional as it sounds. It is just designing lockers☺.

Anyway, Laura's little sister is turning three soon and Laura herself is going to be 14 in a few weeks in September. Then I am turning 14 during the Christmas holidays. Wait... Is Christmas heading over to us or are we heading over to it? Anyway, today, I am so excited because Mom, Lilly, and, I are going to have a long journey from here to London because Tillie (my big sister) has just given birth to a baby boy called Raphael, and we need to attend a kids' fashion competition. Our nieces (also known as "double trouble") will be there too.

I have finished packing now and I have a small cabin bag; so does Lilly. We only have a small cabin bag with us because we do not want to have to go through the long security check-in at the airport. Every time we do, we miss our flight and end up going on a different flight and wasting a lot of money and time. Mom has a medium-sized cabin suitcase, which I am sure will end us up in that security section☹.

***

Okay, so now it is 45 minutes later, and we did not have to go through the boring part, which Lilly and I were happy about. Anyway, the plane just took off 17 minutes ago and Lilly puked ALREADY! In addition to that, Mom made me go with her to the toilet. It looked horrible as well as stunk, and my precious eyes are NOT worthy of looking at such a mess!

Then the crummy flight assistant came round with snacks: Lilly wanted some, but when Mom said no, she squealed and cried until she got her way (it was so embarrassing). So, we bought her peanuts and *kiddie juice*. Bad idea! She needed the toilet again, but she did not puke. Instead, she did a big, fat, and splodgy poop. Actually, ewww (I know what you are thinking; too much info there, Kasey)! It should be illegal to make your 13-year-old daughter see poo and puke in such manner!

Then, for the moment of freedom and glory, the plane landed. Oh wow, now we were in the UK, and I was so excited! We landed at London Heathrow Airport and a taxi called "Uber" was there to take us to the hospital for a limited amount of visitor time. We were meeting our cousins there who were also competing in the fashion event.

When we arrived at the hospital, we immediately went into Tillie's room. Lilly screamed at the sight of Tillie and baby Raphael! Tillie and her husband were very excited to see us, and so were we. Afterward,

Lilly and I went to wash our hands in the toilet, where we met our two cousins, Elsie and Rosie, who were also washing their hands (what an awkward place to find your cousins).

Our parents arranged the same hotel without even telling us☺! Later, it was time to go. Lilly and I went in Rosie's big brother Louis's car, whilst our parents went in the other car. Louis had to drive the car behind his mom's since he didn't know the way. Lilly and Rosie sat in the middle of the car. Elsie and I sat in the back, while Louis sat in the driver's seat. We had a great time making friends and catching up with news and other stuff.

Louis actually planned to sneak off to Chester restaurant. However, since Mom was on face time with me the whole time AND we did not know the way around the city, our plan rather backfired. Then we were all stuck in traffic. It was soooo busy, hot, and stuffy; plus we were sweating gallons! When we eventually arrived at the hotel and got to our suite, it was gorgeous. That was obvious because we all had spent a FORTUNE on it.

We had to go to sleep early because we had the "Kidz competitor's camp" the next day. But at least we got a tiny walk around the hotel with my Uncle Dermot (Elsie's dad). I had to say it was very good. Notwithstanding, Louis said the only fun part was when we got a drink and got a chance to watch the TV. Well, N.O.P. (not our problem). I sure like the British accents around here. Time to put the pen down. Night!

"Ahhhhh, Lilly!" She had opened the curtains when she knew I was sleeping right by them. What a great way to start the morning. NOT☹! I trudged out of bed, headed to the bathroom, and brushed my teeth with Elsie. We took a bath in the large marble bath and by the time Mom, Dad, Auntie, and Uncle were awake, we were dressed. "Time to hit British punk world!" Lilly said. Okay, super cringy. Lilly, we are AMERICANS. Britain is not a world, and we are NOT crusty old punks! I just hope that soon all our British pics virally leak throughout Instagram!

Breakfast was double embarrassing! Lilly was slurping hot chocolate loudly, being silly with food. Rosie was pretty much the same, spilling juice all down her top and sticking her hands into the jam (everyone was staring). But I had a proper English breakfast for the first time, like proper, proper English HOOPLA 😊

CHAPTER TWO

THE KIDZ COMPETITOR'S CAMP

By the time we got there, we had to fill in a whole load of forms to enter. I realized that some kids did not get through, and I was REALLY worried! And Lilly, oh, she was a control freak. She totally blurted out all sorts of gibberish things, at a fast pace and in a high-pitched voice, that I could not understand. "Calm down, Lilly," I interrupted. "We'll be fine," I reassured her.

"Do you truly promise, Kasey?"

"Of course!" I said, foolishly. BIG MISTAKE, I was acting like a fortune teller or something! "What are we, Lilly? Go on, say it," I said, giving her a nudge.

"We are the fashion punks of America!" she shouted. My face had a sudden cringe attack.

No, not PUNKS, Lilly, I said in my head.

When we finished with the forms, we peacefully passed through the security. We then informed the security group organizer about our group number and names. He let us through and said our logo was neat. How sweet of him to say that. When we looked around, we saw all sorts of cool kids with their friends and they'd bought all sorts of cool stuff. It did not really surprise me because I bought my roller boots that could light up and Lilly bought her wheelie shoes (even though they are so 2013). Elsie and Rosie just bought a pair of 'sassy-jay' heeled boots each. Louis did not come, but he did a great job making our lunches.

The announcer said a bunch of stuff that no one really bothered to listen to. My body tingled as everybody screamed; my heart was pumping like MAD. Everyone was put into groups of four and participated in different modeling activities at a time. Jennifer (a kidz rock camp worker) accompanied us. She was nice. Our group (#43z) had to go to the material shop first. Lilly paid for us since she has loads of money; that is all that is important to her. Anyway, I really liked Jennifer. She loved all of us; she did not judge our style and she gave us loads of handy tips☺!

When we came out of the shop department, we went to our workspace. Next, we started to rummage through the bag of clothes. With a bit more time and care, we glued, stitched, cut, stuck, ripped, and put all our energy into making props for the final show. We had a lot of trouble with the glitter gun and Lillie accidentally cut her entire nail off. There were shouts, screams, and blood everywhere, and poor Jenifer had to run around sorting everything out. But, at the last minute, although we were covered in messy model supplies, our designs were totally hitting the fashion nations! So, we took a break and grabbed lunch then moved on to our next two activities.

As soon as everyone assembled for lunch, I quickly sketched out some more designs (just in case of an emergency). Lillie got the whole budget sorted for us! This was certainly a great start for our business, and I had already finished making our website. We were already on the move, ready to get started with a mini-career of our own. But there was one problem: Lillie. She was getting too overexcited, and I was a bit worried in case she started getting a bit 'tooooo' over the moon and started spreading gossip about our business. Then my whole job would get stolen, someone would take Lilly's money, AND the whole thing would get looped! Ok, I need to calm down. What could go wrong? Unfortunately, ANYTHING could go wrong ☹.

Well, anyway, the competition went well. There were 123 people there. We didn't come first, second, or third. We made it to the top twenty. We nearly even earned a press conference with Zendaya Coleman, which was good too. And, my mini-career won't be so bad after all. But we were quite bummed to find out we didn't even get the 3rd place ☹. Hey, come on, even the security guard said our designs were neat!

CHAPTER THREE

RACING AGAINST TIME

We now get timed for almost everything

because of our new teacher. She is always like

chop chop, clap clap; we are not children

anymore. Well, I'm pretty sure we all know that we are teens now. She always says the same thing—we need to race against time. It could be quite stressful, like when we are doing a test and we are trying very hard. She is called Mrs. Timlinson, but we all call her Mrs. Timeline😊.

She is so obsessed with being on time that if we have to, say, beat a goal of fifteen minutes, in the last few seconds, even before the time is up, she starts going, "Come on … you'll lose" or, "Come on, it's the last few minutes, look at the time… It's nearly this … it's nearly that." Then I start stressing and hurrying, then I get everything wrong, and I start to get tired and worried that I will not finish up on time.

I also have to put up with two new weird twins called Mollo and Pollo. I know what you are thinking, right? DOUBLE TROUBLE alongside my twin nieces ☹! Also, surprisingly, when I got home, Lilly said that she wanted me to come to have a chat in her room about her new show. And she most clearly said a LITTLE WORD, but I ended up staying in a luxurious celebrity show land, planning stuff and recording... It was so much fun. I can't believe she has her own TV show! One ~~small~~ ~~BIG~~ gigantic problem! If my family becomes famous and everyone knows about my scrummy life then I'll be bullied until college☹!

I spent a whole hour in there; Lilly's room was so cool: it had cameras everywhere, microphones, and even costumes and props. We were behind the scenes of *Lilly Days*, which is Lilly's new TV show. Her room has been expanded and her bed was in a mini prop station. I asked if I could get a little credit too, but she stuck a tongue out and said, "No way, Kasey!" She is so RUDE. Besides, how is my little sister supposed to be famous without me earning some fame too?

I was quite impressed with Lilly until she said that she could not pay for my budget for my job. So I was puzzled and then said, "But you have a lot of dollars and cents. Can't you even lend me a few cents and then I will earn the rest for myself?"

"NO you don't deserve it!!" she snapped. So, I just wandered off and slouched, and I put on my saddest face for her to have pity on me, but she just stood straight, folded her arms, and gestured with her other arm for me to go out. Can somebody tell me, how did little kids start ruling the world and since when?

Anyway, I entered my room with some ideas for how I could earn some bucks. After a few minutes of searching through my box of junk, I decided to do a skin productive sale. I headed off to the bathroom with empty bottles and cosmetic containers and filled them with all different soaps and body lotions—even though I didn't make them. Oh well 😊. I then 'borrowed' some of my mom's bath bombs (although I never asked) and was brave enough to go around the neighborhood and sell; surprisingly, I earned $35. I thought that was enough for the day. I could earn the required budget tomorrow.

So I decided to go to bed and I drifted off to sleep. Only after what seemed like a few seconds, rays of sunlight shone into my eyes. For goodness' sake, it was Lilly AGAIN! She opened the curtains AGAIN. Well, I guess it was time to rise and shine because today's Sunday. SUN day (no pun intended) 😊.

After church service, we went for a roast at 'Winston George's house'. I did not really eat that much because I was stuffed with bacon, sausages, pancakes, and cheese omelets earlier on. Hey, it tasted good!

Whilst we headed home, I started figuring out prices for some lush samples instead of just selling already made soaps. I did need to earn a few more bucks so it was worth thinking of. So, once that was sorted, I asked Mom if I could head over to Alisha's house (she's the best when it comes to cosmetics). So, Mom dropped me at her house and everyone was already there waiting for me. "Aren't I early today?" I said sarcastically. Then we all completely burst out in laughter. "Okay, I've got the prices down," I said whilst waving my clipboard in their faces.

"And my mom is coming to bring the ingredients in!" Chloe yelled.

Suddenly, Chloe's mom came in with all sorts of different colored liquids and powders and plumped them into the bathroom. However, before we could even move a muscle, we had to put on our "safety" kits. Next, we charged into the bathroom. It was so fun! We mixed different powders and liquids together and then added different scents to each of them. We made masterpieces. We had to clean up afterward because we made a big mess. Surprisingly, we earned lots of money. However, we had to share it between us all.

When I got home, I decided to phone Victoria, one of my distant friends from kindergarten school. I spent half the night speaking to her and we had a big never-ending discussion about daily upcoming events like Christmas and New Year's Eve. Even though the chat was good, unfortunately, Mom had to spend a lot of money on the phone bill. Sorry Mom, but having a teenage girl is very expensive, you should have thought about it BEFORE I was born😊.

"ZEET, ZEET!" Uugh my alarm! I stretched my arm out, waving it around to try to turn it off, but I could not see it when I was half-asleep. Obviously not. And then there was a loud BOOM. I quickly opened my eyes and looked out the window. It was the mailman with my post package!!!! I raced downstairs, almost tripping over my own slippers, and slung the door open. "Hello, sir. Yes, I know it's here," I squealed. The man passed it to me, and I ran away into my room with it.

When I took it out, my whole new school outfit was there. "MY SCHOOL OUTFIT'S HERE!!!" I sang over and over again, holding it in front of me like I was wearing it. I could soon hear Dad's footsteps approaching my room. So, I headed to my bathroom and brushed my teeth, showered, and immediately changed.

Once I was changed, I was so in the mood for golden buttered and smoky toast. So, I stuffed all my breakfast in my mouth and put more and more buttery toast in my already chubby belly. Then I left without saying goodbye to anyone and skipped all the way to school without speaking to a single soul. Laura's and Sophie's new outfits had come too. I kind of felt bad the way we bragged to Linda, but Laura said not to mind a single cupcake. So, I don't feel quite bad about myself after all.

Everyone except Diana forgot their homework: the diary entry assignment for firework night, even though firework night had long since passed.

She wrote this:

Its dark, dull, and loud irritating sounds make your guts shake with sickness (which is why I just stayed at home). No one likes firework night; it is boring.

She was sent to detention during lunch and it didn't look like she cared an inch. I wonder how her parents raise her. I've had a play date with her before, and I had to promise not to spill words out to a single body. But I have to say, compared to my room, her room is ridiculously evil! Diana's wallpaper is black; she has a dead bat that she locks in a cage. At the corner of her room lays a tiny red lamp. Her radio is too loud. She has disturbing comics all over the floor, and she has inappropriate pictures of pop stars on her bunk bed. Her room is also very small. I do not like Diana's room at all. I could even let out an everlasting moan about her room.

Moreover, what we ate for lunch was inappropriate and against the law!!! We ate ham, potatoes, peas, and tuna mixed together inside a moldy piece of sandwich. The only acting I remembered was Mom stammering,

"Err-erm … I-I'm err… Thank you for the food, Mr. and Mrs. Batson, err … we shall be going now, bye." And my dad just posed a cheesy smile and screwed up his face.

CHAPTER FOUR

EARNING CHRISTMAS FAME
(NOT MUCH REALLY)

I got home that night and decided to record a new video for my new artistic themed YouTube channel and the theme will be room decorating for Christmas. So, I made little plastic snowflakes and stuck some shiny papers on them and hung them from my ceiling. I glittered my walls up and added fairy lights to the walls too. I got a little cardboard box and covered it in cotton wool and glue then added Lilly's dolls on top for them to sit down. Later, I even created winter clothes for them and cut off a plastic shovel and tied string to it to make a limited-edition sledge to put one of her dolls on. I also made a winter mansion for all three of the dolls to fit in. I then got my bubble machine and switched it on so the bubbles could be snow.

When Mom saw what I had created, she said it was a miraculous winter wonderland. I posted it all over different social media sites too. Lilly's room was great too. She bought book-sized Christmas trees and decorated them with pipe cleaners and made tiny balls from unwanted sweets that I could have eaten.

That very night, I walked over to my window. *It's getting really dark,* I thought to myself and decided to take a look at my calendar. It's only two more weeks till Christmas and my birthday! Christmas is my favorite day of the year because my birthday is on that very day. So I get double presents and double dinners, and all my family and friends come over to celebrate. We go to sleep at 4:00 a.m. and sleep the entire next day. I totally love my birthday and I love myself!

I really wanted to get to bed and have a deep winter sleep until I heard Dad's footsteps coming, and they were sounding as if he was coming close to my room. Then… "STRIKE!" A flash of lightning struck my bedroom window and this part of the story is confusing. "Aah!" I screamed. "It flashed through the window into my eyes!"

Then "Aah!" Dad roared in shock, and then a glass dropped and coffee spilled everywhere.

Lilly peed on herself and my bedroom window was cracked, and it was raining on my new calendar. I had to save it. I ran and snatched it off a hook whilst, somehow, my night bottoms were stuck to the wall, and I was soaked with rain.

In addition, when I managed to get off the hook, my pyjama bottoms ripped open, and I started to cry. I was so confused. I just stood there crying and almost peed on myself like Lilly! This time of our life was so confusing for my family and me. Then, when Mom called our insurer, two police cars, five insurance cars, a fire-truck, and three ambulances came!

I had to sleep in Lilly's room and had to have two eye tests done and eventually had to take some bitter-tasting antibiotics. When I was sleeping, Lilly kept pulling on my covers, so I obviously had to pull her covers back. This went on until Lilly snitched on me. "MOM!" she wailed, "Kasey's snatching the covers off me!" Mom, instead, actually told Lilly to sleep on the floor in the sleeping bag. I was shocked because I was the oldest; it was my responsibility to look after Lilly, and I am the one who usually ends up lying on the floor.

Just then, I heard Lilly starting to cry. "Lilly, are you okay?" I whispered thoughtfully.

"No, because of you, you big lump head," she whined whilst crying.

I had no choice but to kindly guide her into talking about it gradually and emotionally. In fact, it was so emotional that we both cried. So, I got four chairs and arranged them so that there were two chairs in each row, facing one another. I then spread the bed cover over the chairs and stuffed some pillows inside. Then Lilly and I just cuddled up inside the homemade camp for the rest of the night whilst Mom and Dad argued, and things were getting sorted out.

We both just literally sat there hugging tightly and swaying back and forth quietly and actually drifted off to sleep at about 2 o'clock in the morning. "AAAaahh!!!" I screamed. I had just had the worst dream ever.

"Are you okay, honey?" Mom asked whilst coming to me with a tray of coffee and chocolate chip cookies.

"No," I mumbled and let out a big cry, which was like soooo everlasting. Then, after letting out a big cry that seemed like it lasted for a million years, I carried on sniffling. "No, I'm not okay. My eyes are sore, my back is as stiff as a board, my eyes are swollen, my throat is croaky and stingy, and my cheeks feel like balloons compared to my banging head."

"Oh, dear, darling, let's just hopefully see how you get on," whispered my mom.

You know what? Whenever my mom treats me like this, I feel a whole lot better than before, which makes me feel very good. Therefore, I slouched off the pillows and stumbled my way to the toilet to rinse my face... *OH, NO, MY FACE!* My eyes had red rings around them, my lips were dried, and my face was pale.

I quickly poured a large amount of soap on my face towel and scrubbed my face really hard. Then I quickly rinsed it with hot water. Next, I rubbed lotion around my eyes and added a bit of foundation powder on top just to cover me up. Then I rubbed my lips with a lip scrub.

Once I was changed, I headed downstairs, grabbed a marshmallow bar, checked to see if anyone was watching and then ran out with it all the way to school. I absolutely love the taste of the marshmallow bar; the melted marshmallows are gorgeous. Then I ran as fast as I could until I was near the school and I stopped. Oops, I accidentally bumped into Eliza who was with Brittany and her bratty gang.

I quickly, but nervously, said hi and handed them a party invitation. It really is not my fault, Mom made me do it. Obviously, if I had a choice of who I could invite, I would not invite the popular, bratty girls. "Well, Kasey, that's not a very good way to say hi. You just bumped into my new designer `Kellie' shoes," said Eliza.

I got really annoyed by that. But I remembered what Mom always says: "Never be afraid and have the courage to stick up for yourself."

I was really inspired at that moment. "Well, I'm sorry, but you just stood there whilst I was trying to hand something to you, and you knew I wasn't looking," I said defensively, but in a nice way.

"Well, I just bought these designer shoes yesterday and this is the first time I am wearing them!" she shot back rudely.

I got even more inspired by every word Eliza said. "I understand why you got them yesterday, the price was reduced by 80%." I laughed hard. I didn't touch her, but I won the speaking battle.

Then I walked over to Laura and a crowd of others who were huddled around something in a circle. I needed to see what was going on. "What in the world is happening?" I exclaimed. When I finally pushed my way through the crowd, I saw Katelyn; Lewis had offered to take her to my party... AND he had given her a little invitation to his Valentine's pool party, even though that was like next year. I mean, how sweet is that! Katelyn's friendship with Lewis is so cute, it is almost puppy love! I wish I got along with Blake like that.

Just then, our first lesson started; it was MATHS. Oh, no! By the end of the day, I was given a spelling test in which I managed to score 11/20. I agreed to shop for party outfits with my BFFs of course; Brittney and her popular gang came too. Wait… Does that mean I am officially famous? Probably. I was always number one in elementary school. I was the special, talented, kind, and famous Kasey in kindergarten too, but what has happened to me now? I am guessing Brittney used to be a dork in her elementary school.

"Come on, Kasey, dream-jerk, focus," demanded Brittney. Then she, Eliza, and Maddy started giving me unnecessary fashion tips.

This, however, perked me into my senses. Maddy had the worst fashion style ever. The way she dresses, I would say, is disgusting! She could not even dress for her life! So, that's when I totally lost it and yelled, "Maddy, yeah, thanks for the info. NOT. You can't even dress for toffee yet your mom styles all those little woolly jumpers and jeans for you, so puu-LEAZE, I don't need any of your woolly information because it's 'soo' not necessary right now. But, thanks hon, and by the way, I love your woolly choker. NOT!"

Brittney and Eliza shrieked with laughter; everyone did … except for Maddy. She stood there with fists clenched, and her face was flushing scarlet. So was her brunette hair; you could practically see flames sticking out her head. "You just got beat by a loner!" screeched Eliza, they all held out their cell phones and recorded the scene.

Brittney shrieked with laughter, gave me a hug, and said, "Kasey, you're now officially on the fame platform!"

I stood there speechless. I could not believe what I heard. "Come on, it's only a bit of fame, isn't it?" She rolled her eyes. I nodded automatically, straight away. "Come on then, let's go! Anyone with me?" Brittney asked.

"ME!" we all screeched then rushed off. We tested make-up samples, and we picked some summer clothes for next year. Even though we will have to wait for ages until then, Brittney doesn't have to. She is going to Tenerife, and it will be sunny there. She also said she'd ~~ask~~ BEG her dad if I could come too. I was so excited! Could I be dreaming? No.

I quickly gave myself a pinch on the shoulder to make sure I wasn't dreaming, and YES, I was wide awake. Brittney was being so nice. She was sort of becoming my BFF. I was so lucky, and I mean so L-U-C-K-Y. Then Laura nudged me and gave me a grin. I just shrugged and tried to put on a really nonchalant face, even though I was having a severe attack of B.F.B. (bouncing-fizzy-bubbles) on the inside.

Since we were all tired and starving, I insisted on going to Arby's. We sat down and munched into our burgers and fries. Laura ate two more quarter-pound burgers with another pack of large fries. I could barely eat even though I was the one who insisted on having food. I just could not believe that, after several years, I was going to be the popular, talented Kasey again.

I only managed to chew three fries and I didn't even eat my burger. So Laura asked for it and downed it all!

And then, can you believe it? She went AGAIN and took ANOTHER cheeseburger. That friend of mine will never get full, whilst Brittney ate in a really posh manner and perfectly finished hers.

I just could not get out of my mind that I was myself again! YEAH, right now, my B.F.B. level was to the top or maybe … hhm … over the moon! By the time we left the Arby's, Laura had had her sixth cheeseburger.

We then headed off to the dress shop where we found so many beautiful dresses. There were tutus, tiaras, relishing gowns, and more... I picked the most beautiful and prettiest dress in the entire universe. It lit the whole shop up (okay, maybe NOT the whole shop). I probably did not need a light at home anymore or … wait for it… I COULD BE THE DISCO

BALL FOR MY PARTY☺! But the dress was too expensive and maybe a bit over the top. As a result, I ended up buying some frilly ripped jeans and a really nice top.

Then someone poked me on the shoulder and said, "Come on, miss, you can wonder all you want, but you are not at home, okay?" It was Brittney. I don't know why I always have to be in such a dream world. OH, NO, stop. I'm starting to dream again. I had all these designer shopping bags and I was confidently walking down the aisle of the shopping mall like a true diva … and I really enjoyed every single bit of it. I felt again like the confident and bubbly Kasey I had always been until now.

I gave myself a good knock on the head to get me back into my senses. "We may as well get dressed and take a selfie to celebrate this girls' evening," Brittney said.

"Yeah, that's true, Brittney. Good idea," we agreed.

That was until she said, "You can just stand back and fan me." So, she wanted US to take a selfie but never wanted US to be in the selfie.

Thus, we headed off, got changed, and 'we' took a few selfies. We then went to the soda fountain shop and bought strawberry milkshakes with some cream and marshmallows on the top.

Then each of us said goodbye and headed to our homes. I took the bus with Laura and Patricia. They kept on telling me that Brittney was just using me to dump Maddy and make me popular. So, I said, "How do you know that Brittney's using me? Besides, you're not mind readers." However, they kept going on and on until I totally lost my mind and yelled, "You know what? I'd rather sleep on Lilly's crusty toenails than listen to you two babbling because I'm about to be popular Kasey again, but you're just trying to make me unpopular because you're probably just … err … JEALOUS, yeah. So, leave me alone. What kind of girls are you? You won't even let your friend BE with her new BFF!"

Suddenly, I felt like someone had just punched me in the stomach, I had hurt my BFFs so badly and they wouldn't even talk to me for the rest of the bus ride. And I was so shocked that the nasty words that I said were repeating in my head. I had called Brittney my new BFF and my actual, true, special BFFs— girls. What was wrong with me? Why did I have to be so mean? It made me hurt even more when I saw Laura's eyes filling up with tears. She was looking at the window so that no one saw her crying. Laura never cried before, so it tore my heart to shreds to see her cry for the first time. What had I done?

When we reached our street, I gave them both a nervous little smile and neither of them did anything or said anything back. Brittney took my arm and told me to ignore them.

That night, I went home and went to the kitchen, took a few sweets, ate them all, went to my room, turned off the light, and cried myself to sleep… Aaah! I had the worst dream ever! I dreamt that when I went out, everyone (including my BFFs) called me a "fake unpopular friend." I gave myself a quick pinch just to make sure it wasn't real, and there I was, in bed. Phew.

Anyway, when I went to school the next morning, Brittney and Eliza grabbed me straight away. I got to take Maddy's seat at lunch and sat at the popular girls' table. Everyone totally praised me; it was the best day ever! But whenever I passed by Laura, Katy, Patricia, and Sophie, they turned their heads in the other direction. But I knew that Brittney, the Queen of Celebs and Coolness was on my side.

***

I continued being their best friends for about two weeks, but I couldn't stand it without my BFFs until I got a really good idea. I really wanted to be the popular Kasey, but I couldn't just dump all my true friends whom I have known for such a long time.

The next day was getting a bit boring until Brittney said, "I know we could do a catwalk show and we could be the hosts for your birthday, Kasey!"

So, I pleaded, "And my best friends will be in it?"

"I thought we were your best friends," said Brittney, puzzled.

"Oh, I meant my other best friends," I said.

"Oh, yes, they can come too or we could do something else … and you make sure that they don't know about it at all. How does that sound?"

I could tell Brittney was getting really impatient with my plan, but she just plastered a large smile on her face and twisted a lock of her curly gold hair around her fingers and said sweetly, "Maybe we could have a personal BFFs section in your party instead?"

"With you and Eliza in it and my other old BFFs," I said smartly, yet innocently.

That's when she completely lost it and yelled, "You know what, Kasey, you smart, little, innocent faker? You might as well go and worship your little friends because you're no longer welcome. KLICK. Go away and live with them, hon. Feel free to, but just know you'll never be coming back at my feet again, young lady. Your fame has now ended!" She said it like she ended a contract or something.

Now I was all lonely for the rest of the week. I didn't just feel like the Kasey I am. I felt as lonely as a lost ant in a gigantic world. I tried everything to try to make my BFFs talk to me, but it just didn't work. I phoned them, but they hung up on me. I texted them, but they never replied. I met them online, but they left me out and played among themselves. I even stayed up all night making them a pop-up 'sorry' card with glitter, acrylic paints, water-cake paint colors, cards, gems, and some necklaces for them to keep. When I handed it to them, they just took it… BUT I cannot bear to write what happened next…

Later on that day, I found the card ripped and inside the garbage bin. The necklaces were there too, all broken. I just could not believe what I saw. I actually felt like calling the principal on them. They even invited Maddy to join them every day at lunch and recess.

Have you had any hard and pressuring times? If you have, please write down what happened below to make me feel alright again.

_____

_____

_____

_____

_____

_____

Thank you for taking the time to search through your memories to write it here. 😊

After writing it here, now I know that if your situation was worse, it is not the end of the world.

Anyway, today was not a good day for me. For starters, I forgot my project homework. Then I got 5/20 in my spelling test because I forgot. Next, I got 16/30 on my math test. Even Eliza scored more than I did.

Afterward, at lunch, Brittney purposely tripped me up and my food went flying everywhere, but luckily it didn't land on me. Instead, of the food spilling all over me, the water spilled all over my jeans, so now it looked like I had wet myself, and everyone laughed, including my BFFs. I was so angry and sad. So

I ran out of the hall and into the toilet, locked myself in and started to cry and scream. It is always the teenage stage in life that is so hard, but I always knew that you have to overcome some obstacles in life.

Anyway, after what seemed like a million years, I felt a lot better than before. In fact, I felt like I had just made a confession to Jesus and he had forgiven me. Then I went to the nearest food machine, bought a chocolate and marshmallow snack bar, and quickly gobbled it down on my way to P.E. It was probably the worst P.E session ever! It was actually a tiresome and unfair lesson.

First, everyone was still going on about what had happened at lunch. Second, no one wanted to be my partner for soccer, so I was put with this strange girl called Celery, and I was getting so sweaty. Ewe! Celery is certainly strange. Her short, lacy hair flops everywhere. She is very tall too. Her round, black glasses make her eyes stick out like owl eyes. In addition, seriously, all she ever talks about is friendship and what her mom cooked for her in her packed lunch.

Then we both got the UN-inflated ball for our two-at-a-timer sports game, and Mr. Armstrong said it was our fault for getting the UN-inflated ball when he was the one who gave it to us. I would have rather babysat my little sister Lilly than done this P.E session, and I say that because she has slap cheeks, and her cheeks are like red balloons.

Later that day, I ran into the toilet, ripped a page out of my precious diary, and wrote quickly but neatly:

To my special BFFs, I know we're not getting along at the moment, but I need you. It's really urgent. I need to speak to you both at our secret meeting place (the archive library). But I understand if you don't want to come.

Love from your best buddy, Kasey.

Then a small tear rolled down my cheek and splashed on the page. I then stuck the letter onto one of my BFF's desk so she would hopefully read it and they would come and see me.

As soon as it was a free period, I went and hid in the secret archive and waited. It felt like it had been forever, so I checked my watch; it was now half past two! I had been waiting for 30 minutes so far. I couldn't believe it! My stomach started to churn, and I started to panic. What if they did not want to see me? What if someone saw the letter and now knew our secret hideout? What if the principal saw it? My stomach started thumping.

Just then, the door opened. It was Laura and Patricia. I stared at them in disbelief, for I thought they would not have come. I did not know how to start off the meeting, so I nervously chewed my lip and said, "Hi, so it is … em … a long time I have not … you know ... spoken to you guys and … I just wanted to say…" Then there was a minute of silence that got broken by me when I blurted out, "I have been so lonely for the past few days and it broke my heart to see you didn't care about the masterpiece card that I stayed up all night to make. I also spent $75 on each one of those necklaces, especially for you guys… But all the same, I'm sorry for what I said on the bus. I was just so carried away, and since I'm your

BFF, I had to come and own up quickly. I'm sorry."

Then I started again. "And I—" But then I was interrupted by Laura who said guiltily and softly, "I'm sorry if we got on your nerves. We weren't jealous. We were just trying to help."

"I'm sorry about that," I said, in a naive voice. I then burst out a river of tears, ALMOST NEARLY MAKING A POOL!

"Oh, come on... turn off the tap," said Laura, and we all had a group hug. I was so lucky to have the best BFFs in the whole universe. I knew I could count on them. Whenever the time, whatever the matter, they're always there for me.

***

So, anyway, about my party, it is only two more days until December. All I need to worry about is how I am going to deal with Brittney and her lot. I think it will settle, but what I am really focusing on is that my BFFs have made friends with Maddy, and we totally dislike each other, AND there is so much going on in my life right now that I haven't even decided yet about the food, decorations, and party stuff.

This year is going to be quite exciting because, this year, my parents said they are not going to deal with anything. So, it is up to me to decide what we are going to do, as long as it is sensible. I have planned a disco, so last week, I got a cheap disco ball from the Dollar Tree store. Hey! I only had 10 dollars on me. Therefore, now all I need to focus on is the food and setting. So, since today was the last day before the Christmas holidays, I called my BFFs—Chloe, Alisha, Patricia, Laura, Sophie, and Katy—over to my house to help me sort out my party.

It was very hard to choose a theme for the party because we all had different ideas. Chloe wanted a fashion party, Alisha wanted a retro party, Patricia wanted a Christmas disco, Laura wanted a giant candy party, Sophie wanted a spa party, and Katy wanted a party with loads of limos. In the end, we put all our ideas together (well sort of). Consequently, it was going to be a disco with a candy buffet, and there would also be retro props. The dress code was Christmas Bratz style.

Well, I am sure my parents will let me dig out a few dollars from them. In addition, I will probably be able to earn more money to buy some pizzas and desserts. Thinking about that, it reminded me of the dinner we were having. Mom made us homemade lasagne, which she makes when she cannot be bothered to cook. All she does is: she melts cheese, mixes it with Doritos and BBQ sauce, and chucks it in the oven.

As we all tucked into our delicious dinner, we discussed the party ideas with my mom and she agreed to them... However, it is all up to me and my BFFs to clean up; we're going to be paid 10 dollars each for that. I know it was not that much, but at least it was more cash for me!

CHAPTER FIVE

NOT AN EARLY BIRTHDAY TREAT!

So, after all the recent drama, I was glad to take a break, and I got even more excited when I was invited to Katy's birthday party. Woo! However, my big sister, Tillie, was very ill, and my mom, dad, and Lilly are actually on holiday for a week. Sounds okay, right? Until the news broke that I had to look after my two nieces for that WHOLE time! Come on! I, at least, wanted to babysit Raphael, but he's too small to be away from his parents. I do not think I have told you this, but Raphael has two seven-year-old big sisters, Ava and Eva. I do not write much about them because they spoil my diary's reputation, which is already quite ruined.

Anyway, they are what you call 'double trouble' or two in a pack of one. Nonetheless, the day came, and I could just smell disaster heading my way. When I took the twins to the

Burger Hut for Katy's birthday, I was soooo embarrassed. All of Blake's friends were there and my BFFs were there too. I was just so shocked to see how everyone adored them so much, EVEN BLAKE! Laura and Chloe actually almost forgot about me.

That was fine, but then it got soooo off the plot when I was talking to Blake. Ava squirted BBQ sauce ON MY SHOE! Then Eva started asking Blake embarrassing questions. And that was when I heard the most embarrassing, ludicrously bizarre words come out of Eva's mouth: "Hey, Blakey boy! Here is a bit of advice. If you want to get on with Kasey, you have to cope with the hairy bush jungle growing in her underarms, even though she shaves it all the time!"

I was like, "Oh, no. She did not..." I could NOT believe she could blurt personal stuff out in public like that!

I could even tell that some strangers nearby started smirking. Blake tried to help, but it just got worse. I locked myself in the restroom and stayed there for about five minutes, cleaning my shoe. I looked like a total clown! As I confidently marched out of the restroom, I grabbed the two troublemaking twins. "Uugh!" I had enough of those two. I did not retaliate. I gently said, "A little accident made, darling, never mind."

Then I dramatically checked my watch. "We ought to be going now," I said poshly. I then grabbed them, tightly squeezing their tiny little wrists, and sprinted out.

"Hey, wait, you're leaving so early... Come back," shouted Katy. But I did not stop once.

Laura was a fast sprinter, and before I knew it, I could feel her chasing behind me. I ran faster this time, like a maniac, squeezing in and out of people so she could not see me. Finally, I lost her.

I squeezed on the twins so much that they cried like thunderstorms. One woman even stopped by and said, "Are you okay? Where are your parents?"

"These are my nieces, not yours. So just back off!" I scoffed.

"Well, someone's in a bad mood today," she muttered to herself.

(Ping) I looked up at the sky. (Ping) A drop of rain fell on my nose. It was dark, and it started raining heavily. I did not stop sprinting until we reached home.

Tillie had left a note on the hallway table saying "Do not let the twins have anything before lunch, breakfast, or dinner. Hugs and kisses, big sis xxx."

Hm? Home alone, I thought to myself. I marched upstairs not caring about what the twins did. I lit candles, put some of Tillie's fizzers in the bath, locked myself in, and dived into the hot bubbling bath. I tried calling Alisha to come over and help me babysit the twins, but she was unable to help as she had family coming over.

Subsequently, after I got dressed and out of the bath, I called Chloe. She is always free. Yep, I was right. I worked a charm. However, it was still very tough even with her around.

"Okay, dinner time," I said.

"No," they screamed, with each mouth filled with crisps.

"Uugh, you know no snacks are allowed before dinner, right?" I was going to be in big trouble if Mom and Dad found out. "You're supposed to be eating tuna sandwiches," I said in an impatient tone. They both shouted that they wanted crisps. I angrily flung the pink plastic plates at them. "Now eat them, you goblins," I yelled.

"No," they shot back.

"Yes," I replied.

The twins both ended it with a screeching, "NO, NO, NO!"

"Look, girls, why don't we pretend to be kittens? I'm sure they love tuna," said Chloe.

Then Ava, the smart one, answered back, "But cats don't eat bread. Plus, they eat raw fish." Chloe told them to use their imagination. They ate up every bit of food on the plate and chorused, "FINISHED!" They started acting as if nothing happened, cooing, "Cwoe is de best, and she is bewy, bewy nithe," meaning, Chloe is the best, and she is very, very nice. I just rolled my eyes. I had had enough of that pathetic nonsense already.

The rest of that evening was mostly just drama. Eva was strutting around in Mom's high heels and makeup, wearing shorts and a tight half-tank top. Ava was crawling around in pyjamas and a pacifier, pretending to be a bad baby. I had to admit, even though Eva was bad at make-up, she looked quite cute with her gold clouds of hair swishing past her tiny bottom. Ava looked cute, too, but gave me a headache. Well, that was that for the night, not to mention we slept after midnight.

Next morning, as a result of us going to bed so late the previous night, we woke up late: at half-past ten. Oh, no! That was just the time Mom told me to go and do some grocery shopping. We had to rush. Ava and I were soaking wet, diving in and out the shower and closet, putting on anything we could find. However, we still ended up late because Chloe and Eva decided to take their time to dress cutely: they wore kitten headbands, flowery shorts, and designer mini boots. The lot! Oh, come on, you know I would give anything to go shopping looking like Wengie.

However, right now, I'm a responsible, good babysitter. So, when my parents come home, perhaps I will earn some extra cash! Anyway, we had to waste about ten more minutes because I had to scrub off Eva's 'morning layer of make-up', which was more like a pig's face on fire if you asked me. This time, she even stuck false lashes on too! I was like, "WOW, good job." But, then again, she still looked cute☺.

At about one o'clock in the afternoon, our shopping in Riverbanks was a disaster but a completely different story. Afterward, to cool things down, I suggested we go to the café to get some brunch. I wanted the special bacon balm. I was lost in thought, thinking about the crispy, sizzling bacon on gold, succulent melting butter covered in the freshest, bouncy, and soft balm. Then Eva and Ava suddenly interrupted me, whining about how THEY wanted to go to the famous soda fountain. THEN... Chloe started whining, too, as if she was a six-year-old. Finally, I gave up and we went there instead.

Well, wrong decision, Kasey! That just made things complicatedly worse. Irrespective of whether it's a real word or not, it's the right word for what happened next. Ava spilled whipped cream all over her and looked like an abominable shaving foam monster! People around us started staring, not to mention Chloe started to order an endless supply of doughnuts. Before you knew it, all three of them were gobbling the doughnuts like mindlessly greedy but cute pigs.

Then Ava started screaming about getting some new clothes. Out of topic. The drama does not end until they finish babbling about this 'Kandy kidz' play area somewhere in the mall. I felt like stuffing those kids into a three-in-one pram. Chloe (**#missbrattyextratwin**) was meant to be helping me rather than becoming my third niece. After that, I thought we all calmed down a bit, so I left them in 'Kandy Kidz' play area for an hour whilst I headed off to get the bacon balm I yearned for. Surprisingly, I ate four of them all by myself. They were so yum! 😊 After eating a few more (I couldn't help it), I went back to the play area... JUST TO REALIZE THERE WAS NO SIGN OF CHLOE AND THE TWINS!?!?

I scanned carefully around the room a few more times. Still, they were nowhere to be seen. I knew Chloe was with them, but it still wasn't safe because she was acting like a baby too! Suddenly, my stomach felt tight and bubbly. I staggered about, clutching my tummy. "Please stay settled, brunch, please stay," I prayed.

I did not know if my food was going to obey me or splat all over the polished floor. Either way, I had to run to the toilet and be sick. But as I was staggering out of the cubicle, I noticed three familiar bubbly heads in the *Koho Doll Shop*, pouring over a life-size Blythe doll. Moreover, I wasn't surprised to see the twins (or now triplets) Eva, Ava, and their newborn sister, CHLOE!

I was so relieved but worked up inside at the same time, Uugh! "Hey, could I join you guys?!" I said coldly. It made them jump. "Chloe! You were supposed to help me, NOT become my third little niece!" I screamed. There was literally fire shooting out of my head.

"We're sorry," they all babbled, batting their lashes and pouting at me. It made me feel utterly grossed out, and it just made me rocket on. "Just stop this nonsense!"

"First, you're winding me up, and I let you come shopping with me when you could have just stayed home. Then I took you to the soda fountain and that silly little *Kandy kidmania thing..."*

"Err... it's Kandy Kidz Kingdom," they cooed as they ALSO interrupted my sentence.

"Look, whatever. I don't care about what it's called, especially if YOU didn't care and you sloped off here without telling me!"

I was so mad that I did not even know that other people were looking at me, neither did I care. So, I nagged on and on anyway. "Plus, Chloe, I called you here to help, and here you are turning yourself into my two nieces' triplet. That *is soooo not happenin' sista!"*

Later on, as I did not want to be the one who spoilt the shopping, I composed myself. Since my breakfast ended up in the toilet earlier on, I took the twins and Chloe to "the 5-star bacon bap" shop 😋. I only ate one… Okay… I couldn't resist another one; the time came when I had to control my hunger, for I had already wasted my money being sick this morning.

After that, we made our way over to the Topshop. Of course, I did not have any money left, so we tried clothes on instead. That was when I got super creative and we started playing super chic models, spending a few hundreds of imaginary dollars on the most trendy and stylish outfits in town. Right now, it sounds cringy, but it was fun. Chloe got a really chic outfit; I got a casual 'top man' outfit; Ava got a rainbow dress; and, although Eva is only seven, she picked a gold tube top and a really short skirt (I have no idea where this seven-year-old gets this inappropriate sense of dressing from) 😊.

After an exhausting, stressful morning, we sloped off back home. I then slept for the rest of the day. OMG!!! I felt an awful biting burn in my stomach… OWW! It hurt so badly. I needed to call Mom. I called her. Luckily, she said she might make it home tomorrow evening. YES😊! But that didn't help the fact that I was feeling that I was going to throw up gas; I took some painkillers. OWW! That did NOT work; it was worse. That night, I could not sleep.

At one point, I got so agitated and scared that I suddenly woke up!

I then got a piece of paper and started writing things like:

Are you there?

NOOO!   I miss you, NOOO!

Hellooooo?   Come back!?!

            Are you there?

NOOO!!!   I miss you, NOOO!

CHAPTER SIX

ALMOST TIME

The whole of this morning, I stayed in my

room doing **important** stuff (writing in my

diary). Hey! If I didn't write, YOU wouldn't be

reading all the juicy extracts from MY diary (not

that I want you to know all the private stuff in my life) 😊. Finally, I got out of bed around midday because I was peckish; that was when I spotted a note on the little hallway table. It was quite a long letter; the bold, elegant writing looked familiar. It was from Chloe.

Dear Kasey,

Your mom called and told us about your health; even though at the time you probably did not trust me, you should have told me. The girls and I have decided to give you some space this afternoon. Do not worry about us. I will have them back before the family comes. I will look after them. Sorry about yesterday. Chloe xxx.

That was so kind... AND I have soooo much space to myself today. That's when I decided to roam about in my PJs, watching TV and pigging out on some delicious treats (since my appetite was worked up from yesterday). This afternoon was enjoyable, relaxing and drama-free!

I even put curlers in my hair, some cucumbers on my eyes, ordered pizza and had a mini orbeez spa (it is Lilly's, but I borrowed it).

Now all I needed to do was take a selfie and post it at #bestofalltime😊! After an hour and a half or so, the doorbell rang. *Oh, no. Not the twins!* I thought. Surprisingly, when I opened the door, the twins were calm and happy! However, I could tell Chloe looked ~~quite a bit~~ VERY scrambled and flabbergasted. Poor thing 🙁. What also caught my attention was what was inside the giant shopping bags they were holding. I could slightly see Christmas and birthday bunting.

I was so happy that I decided to trick them. "What have you done?" I said sternly. "Ava, Eva!" I shouted, whilst motioning my finger for them to come towards me. As the frightened twins shuffled towards me, a broad mad smile stretched across my face as I hugged them and tickled them. "Tricked you! Thank you so much!" Then, in the corner of my eye, I saw Chloe awkwardly twitching in the corner of the doorway, looking at the floor and then at us. "And, you, Chloe, you're the one who came up with all of this!"

As she skipped over to join us, I said, "Look, guys, I'm sorry about yesterday; I was just so ticked off and sick. I'm sorry, Chloe. I should have told you about my health," I said.

"It's alright… Friends?"

"YES!!!" everyone screamed.

Since everyone was hungry (except for me, of course), I let them have the rest of the food that was left over.

After another few hours of watching TV, another ring came from the door. It was the rest of the family—including Tillie!

We all ran to the door and waves of excitement could be heard from all over the house. I could tell Mom had been out a lot because she had bags of souvenirs, which were packed with a bunch of colorful things. As we all settled down, we had dinner (Mom's special cob salad served with tater tots and homemade fizzy peach soda). I know my mom is the best chef 😌.

After what I call friends and family reunion dinner, it was time to get our souvenirs. Firstly, we all received "caramelos" (Spanish candy). Next, I got a new pastel aqua and purple mosaic backpack, Chloe got a pair of flamenco girl earrings with a matching bracelet, and the twins got Spanish Barbie dolls for themselves with vibrant colors and sophisticated patterns. OMG! Even though I was no longer a kid, I still LOVED these dolls; they were so cute. Ava would play school with them; Eva would just try to look like them… And me? When I was little, I stayed in my room all day, sticking, stitching, and cutting with a concentrated frown on my face, lolling my tongue about from side to side… I would create miniature doll clothes for them; that's where my love for fashion began.

Whenever I went to Tillie's house, I would always secretly "use" Eva's en suite. I would always stroke the silk embroils, rhinestone leather, and patterns on each doll's dress, creating a color-coded room for them depending on the colors of the dolls' outfits. For example, the Coachella style doll—the walls would be covered in vibrant patterns and rhinestones matching its custom-made feather outfit. Whilst for the very expensive dolls I would create sparkly pink walls and a wide selection of designer pink, black, and white clothes as well as matching barrettes and purses.

On the other hand, more casually, sometimes in winter, I would take them outside and catch snow on our tongues. It filled me with great pleasure and memories of happy times.

Sometimes, I even wished the dolls were my friends and family! I would feel just like a child again. Nothing to worry about and no responsibilities. All you had to do was follow your heart 😊!

Xxx night. P.S. It is my birthday in three days!

***

Morning! Sorry about last night. I was sleepy and fell asleep. Aaaaah! It's school today! Oh, no! ☹.

***

I can't believe I dozed off AGAIN! I jumped here and there to get my school things. I looked like a mad woman! I grabbed my books and papers, rushed downstairs, snatched a breakfast bar from the table and then ran out the door and up the street like a psycho whilst eating. I just still can't get over it. I was soooo angry! I didn't even get time to finish my make-up and my clothes were a "jimble-jamble" (it means unruly, split, and mixed up. I made that word up).

When I finally reached school, not only was I breathless and didn't study for my science test but I was also completely pink! Oh, no... NOT rosy cute pink, but bright, unevenly parted pink! I nearly choked on my breakfast bar when I looked at my face in the mirror; I tried rinsing it with water and scrubbing it with a paper towel, but that just made it beetroot red! Therefore, I trotted to math class twelve minutes late with a pool of sniggering eyes staring up and down at me, as if I was a giant corn dog splattered in pickle sauce or something. I could see the sympathy in my BFFs' eyes.

I got a five-minute lecture about being late as well as coming to Mrs. Chapman's math class in a disorganized manner.

So I shouted, "Hey! I am the fashion hero here. You are the math master, and if there is one combination that does not go together, it's math and fashion (apart from the measurements, but let's just forget THAT part). So, fix yourself before you fix others!" Even though I said it inside my head, it made me feel tons better 😊. Even though this made me feel better, I still had to get over the fact that I had to stay in the library for an extra 15 minutes before my science test 🙁.

Nevertheless, I am just so happy that we FINALLY finish school for our Christmas break today. IT WILL BE MY BIRTHDAY SOON! 😊.
I just cannot wait! Anyway, after a catch up of math class, we had to go to English.

Guess what? I was on my way to my locker when Brittney and her popular gang skipped over and started accusing me of cheating in math. HOW COULD THEY? I mean who do they think they are, going around saying things about me that are soooo NOT true!? Despite this, I invited her to my birthday; this could not be true☹.

Because we were breaking up for Christmas, my birthday☺, we finished school half an hour early today (too much time taken off education - eye roll!). School should have, at least, finished two hours before normal closing time.

Anyway, instead of going home and getting ready for my birthday and chillaxing at home, I had to stay in the library and get lectured for half an hour for coming to school late. At one point, I got so ticked off that I yelled, "Well, hey teachers, guess what you're missing out on? The best birthday Christmas disco, a good life, having friends, and everything in general!" Even though I said it inside my head again, it did make me feel A LOT better. But one thing that I found sweet during this lecturing was that my BFFs were there with me the whole time☺! Who could have better BFFs? NO ONE. I HAVE GOT THE BEST!

As we headed out of the library, I thanked them. "OMG, guys, you're the best. I don't know what I'd do without you!" I gushed.

That was when they all hugged me and said, "True friends are never apart, maybe in distance but not in the heart." OMG! My cold, frosted Christmas heart melted into a sentimental sappy puddle of goodness☺!

As I reached home, we (as in my family) all went to get a Christmas tree from the tree shop; I know it was quite late to go shopping for a tree and decorations, but for my family, it's normal. We always do it on Christmas Eve. Mom wanted one of those cheap small ones, Dad and Lilly wanted a gigantic tree with loads of decorations for the party, and I just wanted to get my shellac manicure already! Obviously, we ended up buying the gigantic one.

Next, we headed to the nail salon and I got a shellac manicure. Lilly and Mom also got their nails done too. They had shellac.

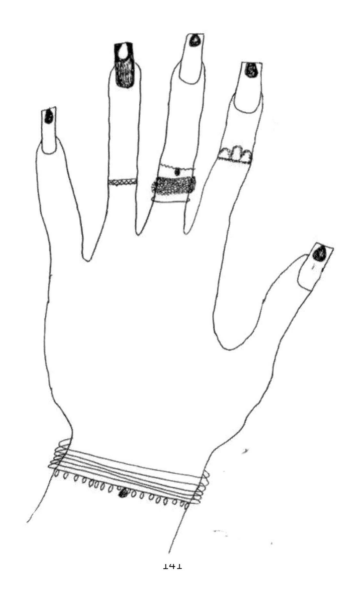

Dad could not stand it, so he took a break at a fast-food shop nearby; he did NOT buy us ANYTHING—he did not even save us a chip☹.
Then we went back home to set up the decorations, and like she does every year, Lilly once again did a great job and knocked the tree over just after we'd spent an endless hour of hard work decorating it. Thanks, Lilly. NOT☹! Anyway, we set up everything and put the party food in the fridge for tomorrow.

Everything was perfect! However, there was one thing that kept bugging me, and I could not sleep. It was something I could not quite put my finger on. Then, finally, in the middle of the night, I woke up and panicked. I had invited Brittney to my party because she was my 'friend'! You are probably thinking, *What is so bad about that?* Well... SHE IS NOT MY FRIEND ANYMORE! Moreover, I knew she would be up to no good, especially when I wanted a drama-free first ever birthday party in years. I quivered about helplessly... What could I do?

I guessed I could just have a not-so-great party after all. That was when the most amazing idea popped into my head. Yes, the best but not the most mature idea. So, I decided to ring Brittney—YES ... at this time (to save my party) and tell her that my party was cancelled due to ... erm ... err ... my severe case of GERD (Gastroesophageal reflux disease). It worked a charm, and because I had missed most of my sleep, instead of calling Eliza, I just sent her a text about the same thing.

***

Today was the day!!!! It was Christmas day AND my birthday. My party did not start until noon, so we went to Gigi and Opa's (our mom's parents) house for a special Christmas breakfast.

The thing I liked was that we were given permission to go in our pyjamas. We ate yummy Santa Claus pancakes and drank red Christmas sparkling lemonade; it was yum. Gigi made it☺. Next it was time for the presents. Even though we were not allowed to open them until my party, I was guessing it was some sports attire or clothes (Gigi is a very sporty grandma. She even has her own hip-hop class☺).

Then we went back home to get ready for the party, which is when my OTHER grandma, Nana Gracie, came to help. She did my hair and make-up, and do not judge too fast! My nana is VERY good when it comes to beauty, she owns the 'Color Me Crazy' beauty salon. Then we got dressed. I just loved how my clothes looked with my hair and make-up!

Shortly after, the guests started to come, ALREADY! First, Patricia, Sophie, Alisha, Laura, and Katy came. I invited them 30 minutes earlier so Nana Gracie could do their very own special makeovers too.

Once we were finished, the six of us posed in front of the mirror; we looked fab-glamorous!

And when the others arrived, we posed for a beautiful photo with my amazing BFFs and my other guests. Brittney and her pratty little gang were a no-show☺! This was cool.

I always thought about Christmas as an extraordinary day for me to get more presents. However, this was not always the case because whenever someone gave me a present, they would say that it counted as both my Christmas and birthday present.

This time, I calculated how I could get double presents from friends and family. It was a VERY long calculation, but I eventually got there and told everyone about it! "Look, I got the following: two presents from Mom + two presents from Dad + two presents from Lilly + two presents from Nana Gracie + two presents from Gigi + two presents from Opa + two presents from each guest (38 in total) = 88 presents!" Yeah☺.

Anyway, there was a mini-buffet, loads of balloons, a giant cake made from doughnuts, and loads of decorations! It was a BLAST. It was the best birthday ever!

Right now, I am very tired, and the party is over. I will catch up on the main details in my next diary entry. But one thing I sure can say, again and again, is that the party would have ONLY been a blast because of what I said when I called Brittney. I literally thought she wouldn't believe me, and I thought she would gatecrash. Every time I heard the bell ring, my gut was doing acrobatics! I am a bit weird... Okay... VERY weird, but it's Kasey-weird: a unique one that no one can steal. Good night☺!

Eliza   Lynda   Britteny   Maddie

Notes

....

....

....

....

....

....

....

....

....

....

....

....

....

WATCH OUT FOR MY NEXT DIARY!

ABOUT KASEY'S DIARY

This is an inspiring story based on a teenage girl called Kasey. She experiences everyday changes and challenges, just like an ordinary girl. But it inspires young girls to be better. Even if you think you are the best, you can always do better, making each new day better than the previous one.

Kasey Anderson is a prominent character and positive role model in Short Stories by Latoya Likambi. This time, she has returned with a whole new adventure! But a twist is added: her self-esteem has dropped significantly … way down to the bottom of the esteem-meter. Nevertheless, her future depends on herself; if her self-esteem increases, then she will inevitably be the best she can be!

Take a deep breath, buckle your seatbelts, and get ready for an unforgettable plane ride with Kasey, soaring through clouds of trouble and dodging through storms of drama. Will she land on her dream birthday cloud? Be prepared to laugh, yawn, and freak out whilst reading.

AUTHOR'S BIOGRAPHY

Latoya Likambi is a highly confident, eloquent, and very inspiring 12-year-old Cameroonian-British from Liverpool. She wrote her first book at the tender age of seven, which she then edited and published when she was 10.

She is a very creative, strong-minded, and visionary young girl, with a vision bigger than the world she sees in front of her. She is grounded by her profound Christian foundation and family values and believes that she and every child out there is a unique creation of God, with very unique and exceptional creative abilities and potential to add value to the world and make it a much better place.

She is the author of *Short Stories by Latoya Likambi*. While in primary school, she won various awards as the best writer of the week and month, got an inspiring poem of hers published in *A Liverpool Talented Writer's* book when she was eight, and has been a reading ambassador and school counselor for her primary school and is currently a school counselor in her school. She has read over 350+ books to date.

She is very passionate about fine art and design and is currently working on her own clothing line and her next book on women's rights, due to be published by August 2019.

Latoya is highly inspired by her mom, Dr. Sylvia Forchap-Likambi, Jacqueline Wilson, and Rachel Renee

Russell and hopes to write a series of books that will be available to read in schools across the country and abroad.

Latoya is available for interviews and to speak at schools or events for young people.

For interviews, further information, and bulk orders:

Contact: Dr. Sylvia Forchap-Likambi

Tel: +44 (0) 75 3921 6072

e-mail: books@likambiglobalpublishing.com

Printed in Great Britain
by Amazon